ODE TO UNDERWEAR

Helaine Becker

illustrated by
Mike Boldt

Scholastic Canada Ltd.
Toronto New York London Auckland Sydney
Mexico City New Delhi Hong Kong Buenos Aires

Scholastic Canada Ltd.
604 King Street West, Toronto, Ontario M5V 1E1, Canada

Scholastic Inc.
557 Broadway, New York, NY 10012, USA

Scholastic Australia Pty Limited
PO Box 579, Gosford, NSW 2250, Australia

Scholastic New Zealand Limited
Private Bag 94407, Botany, Manukau 2163, New Zealand

Scholastic Children's Books
Euston House, 24 Eversholt Street, London NW1 1DB, UK

www.scholastic.ca

The art for this book was done digitally using Corel Painter and Photoshop.
The type was set in 24 point Filosofia.

Library and Archives Canada Cataloguing in Publication

Becker, Helaine, 1961-
Ode to underwear / by Helaine Becker ; illustrations by Mike Boldt.
ISBN 978-1-4431-2475-1
I. Boldt, Mike II. Title.
PS8553.E295532O34 2013   jC811'.6   C2013-901804-2

6 5 4 3 2 1   Printed in Singapore 46   13 14 15 16 17

Let's hear it for our underwear,

Our fun-to-wear best underwear!

It keeps us warm and dry down there,

So give a cheer for underwear!

Panties pink and very lacy,

Jockeys striped, oh so horse-racy,

Those with bows, and those quite sheer,

Those with heroes on the rear!

Boxers, girdles, bloomers, drawers,
All of these your tush adores!

Without them, backsides would be bare,
So say a prayer for underwear!

Plain ones that are big and baggy,

Frayed ones that have gotten saggy,

Purple ones too frou-frou frilly,

Furry ones, frightfully silly!

Every colour, every kind,

Is a friend to your behind.

It's one thing you won't have to share,

So celebrate your underwear!

Briefs, bikinis,
gotch and shorts,

Thermal ones for
snowy sports,

Some that beep,

and some that glow,

Some that shine a
full-moon show!

So grab your very favourite pair,

Wave them high now, if you dare —

Just be sure you have a spare —

And give three cheers for underwear!

I see London, I see France, I see marching underpants!

Undies are often overlooked and underappreciated.
In this laugh-out loud celebration of everyone's
favourite item of clothing, bestselling writer Helaine
Becker and illustrator Mike Boldt get behind briefs,
boxers and bloomers to give them their due.

ISBN 978-1-4431-2475-1

$7.99

90000

9 781443 124751

Scholastic Canada Ltd.